This Coloring Book Belongs to:

....

It is great to have siblings younger than you,
They like to join in everything that you do.

Life's an adventure, it's out of this world,
It's exciting to share with a boy or a girl.

With a younger sibling, you can have a good time,
Laughing together is not a crime.

You can tell funny jokes, make each other laugh,
Did you hear the one about the police car and
giraffe?

We'll have a nice time together for siblings are fun.
We can jump on a trampoline, play games, and run.

You can bounce higher because you are light,
I can't go higher, try as I might.

Sometimes you may argue and disagree,
That's just because you are different to me.

If you feel angry just count up to ten.
We will make up and have fun again,

We love to hear stories when it's time for bed,
We'll read about trains until we nod our heads.

You will sleep first, and then I will too,
It's just because I'm not as sleepy as you.

Discover new places is what you can do,
If you have another sibling with you.

The world is exciting, there's so much to see,
We may even explore under the sea.

Siblings help each other to get hard things done,
Two always make it much easier than one.

So, if you need help, call out to me,
I'll stop what I'm doing and make sure I'm free.

You can share yummy treats, and eat them together,
Inside or outside, it depends on the weather.

Fruit is delicious and good for us too,
So, you share with me, and I'll share with you.

It's always interesting to play with someone,
If it's with your sibling it's even more fun.

We can play outside, just you and me,
Throwing a ball, or climbing a tree.

It is great at the beach when you're with a sibling,
Together you can do sandcastle building.

Use spades and buckets to pick up the sand,
And build the best castles in all of the land.

Pretend you are planes flying to distant places,
Up in the sky, you pull funny faces.

Flying above buildings and shooting through clouds,
Joking around like two silly clowns.

It's great to have someone to play sports against,
Let's kick the soccer ball into the fence.

There aren't many sports you can play alone,
But with a sibling, you can play them at home.

In emergencies, we need someone there,
We must hug our siblings to show that we care.

Protect one another when we're hurt or sad,
If we have a sibling we should always be glad.

It is always good to have siblings close by,
When you're alone you might be sad and cry.

Like buses that can be parked side by side,
Having someone close makes you feel good inside.

When you spend time together you discover new things,
Like playing an instrument, woodwind, or strings.

I'll play the violin, you play the flute,
We are talented musicians, and we're also cute.

Having siblings is a wonderful gift,
Every day they can help make your spirits lift.

So tell them you love them whenever you can,
And they will be your companion and friend.

We hope you enjoy this product.
We'd love it if you could leave a review,
it will help future buyers make a decision.

Made in the USA
Las Vegas, NV
06 October 2023

78618963R00020